THE ZACK FILES

THE INVISIBLE BOY

DAN GREENBURG

Illustrated by
JACK E. DAVIS

MACMILLAN CHILDREN'S BOOKS

For Judith, and for the real Zack,
with love – DG

Copyright © 1998 by Dan Greenburg. All rights reserved.
First published in the United States by Grosset & Dunlap.
British publication rights arranged with Sheldon Fogelman.

This edition published 1998 by Macmillan Children's Books
a division of Macmillan Publishers Limited
25 Eccleston Place, London SW1W 9NF
and Basingstoke

Associated companies throughout the world.

ISBN 0 330 36826 5

Illustrations copyright © Jack E Davis 1998

The right of Dan Greenburg to be identified as the
author of this work has been asserted by him in accordance
with the Copyright, Designs and Patents Act 1988

1 3 5 7 9 8 6 4 2

A CIP catalogue record for this book is available fron the British Library

Printed and bound in Great Britain by Mackays of Chatham plc, Kent

Chapter
One

● ● ● ● ●

You think you've got problems?
I mean, I don't know if you do or not. But if you do think you've got problems, well, they're nothing compared to mine. Not unless you ever got stuck in a parallel universe. Or you had a Hawaiian volcano goddess put a curse on you. Or you ever started turning into a cat.

Oh, I should tell you who I am and all that stuff. My name is Zack. I'm ten and a half and in the fifth grade at the Horace

Hyde-White School for Boys. That's in New York City.

My best friend is named Spencer Sharp. And he is. Sharp, that is. In fact, he's very, very sharp. His IQ is somewhere around 1000. It's cool having Spencer as a best friend. We do just about everything together. Like the time I left my body to do some astral travelling – old Spencer was right there along with me. It was his idea, actually.

It was also his idea to enter Len and Larry's Create-an-Ice-Cream-Flavour Contest together. If we won, we'd get a cheque for a hundred bucks and free ice cream for a year. We would also get our picture in *The New York Times*. That's always been a dream of mine. Fame, fortune, and free ice cream. What more could you ask for?

Spencer and I spent about a million hours trying to come up with cool ideas for new flavours. Here are some of the ones we tried but didn't like:

        Peanut Butter and Jellyfish
        Cashew Cashew Gesundheit
        Chocolate Chimp
        Cow Pies 'n' Cream

And here's what what we finally entered – You Scream Eyes Scream. Our flavour was pretty great, if I do say so myself. It was French vanilla with blobs of blueberry jelly in it. They were supposed to look like big wobbly eyeballs. Then we mixed in streaks of strawberry sauce, like blood. That made it look even grosser. But it tasted great. Honest.

We sent in our recipe about a month ago. Then we sort of forgot about it. We didn't think we had a chance of winning. I mean, would Len and Larry really go for ice cream that looked like it was staring at them?

That's why I was so surprised when I

got a phone call from Len and Larry's on Thursday afternoon. Out of five hundred entries, Spencer and I had made it to the finals. There were five other finalists, too. At first, I thought maybe it was some trick phone call from Spencer. But it was true. A taste-off was going to be held on Saturday at the grand opening of the new Len and Larry's Ice-Cream Parlour. The winner would be chosen right there.

The minute I got off the phone, I started jumping around and screaming like a maniac. This was the most exciting thing that had ever happened to me.

I called Spencer right away. But his phone was busy, busy, busy. So I ran over to his apartment. I couldn't wait to tell him the news. He was just going to die!

By the time I got to Spencer's, I was sweating and out of breath. "Spencer, guess what?" I panted. "I just got a call from some guy at Len and Larry's!"

"Sshhhhh," said Spencer.

Spencer was at his desk. He was carefully pouring something into a test tube and didn't even look up. There were beakers and bottles and glasses all over the place.

"Spencer, we made it to the finals!" I shouted. "We could get our pictures in the paper!"

"Mmmmmm," he said. "Good."

Spencer didn't seem quite as excited as I thought he'd be.

"How come you're not excited?" I asked. I plopped down on Spencer's bed. I was still pooped from running. "We'll also get free ice cream for a year. And a hundred dollars."

"I am excited," he said, in a soft, level voice, never taking his eyes off the test tube. "But I am working on a very delicate experiment here. When I'm done, though, I'm going to holler like a madman."

Spencer continued to stare at the test tube, then swirled it around. "I think my superglue is just about perfect. But I need to put it in the refrigerator. I'll be back in a minute."

"Hey!" I shouted as he left the room. "I'm dying of thirst. You got anything to drink around here?"

"There's lemonade," he called from down the hall.

"Excellent," I said. On his bedside table I saw a glass of lemonade. I gulped some down. Yech! I almost spat it out. It tasted awful.

Then Spencer came back.

"Hey, what's wrong?" he asked.

"Spencer," I said. "I don't mean to be insulting or anything. But that lemonade was the pits!"

"You're kidding me," he said. "I think it's the best pink lemonade I've ever tasted. Not too tart, not too sweet . . ." Spencer went over to his desk and took a sip from a glass.

"Delicious!" he said.

"Pink?" I interrupted him. "Pink lemonade? That's not what I drank. The stuff I drank was yellow."

Spencer's eyebrows shot up. "Oh gosh! Was it on my bedside table?"

I nodded.

He paused for a moment, then took a deep breath. "I don't know how to tell you this, Zack. But you just drank one of my experiments. That wasn't lemonade. It was disappearing ink!"

Chapter Two

● ● ● ● ●

"**D**isappearing ink?" I gulped hard. "Is that p-p-poison?" Spencer shook his head.

"No, of course not. I made my disappearing ink from only the finest, all-natural ingredients. Lemon juice and stuff. Nothing in there can hurt you. And it only works on paper. Want to see how?" Spencer asked.

"Well, sure," I said, feeling very relieved that I was not going to die. "I guess so."

So Spencer got a paintbrush and stuck it

in the glass with the yellow stuff in it. Then he wrote my name on a piece of paper. As the ink dried, my name slowly disappeared.

"Now I'll make it reappear." Spencer turned on his desk lamp. He held the paper up near the light bulb. Slowly I began to see the letters of my name.

"The heat from the light makes the disappearing ink show up again," he explained. "So what do you think?"

"Very cool," I said. "Now that you're done with your experiment – and now I know that I'm not going to die from that disappearing ink – let's get down to business." I rubbed my hands together. "What are we going to do with the hundred dollars from Len and Larry's contest?"

"Don't forget, there are five other finalists," Spencer said. "We only have a $16\frac{2}{3}\%$ chance of winning."

"Oh, don't be such a pessimist," I told Spencer. "You Scream Eyes Scream is delicious. Hey, maybe I should get my hair cut before Saturday." In my mind, I could already see the picture in *The New York Times*. I wanted to look my best. Ater all, someday I could show it to my kids, like my son Mack. (I don't know if I mentioned this before. But I met my future son, Mack, once when he travelled back to the present on a school bus trip.)

"I have a real good feeling about this contest. I feel lucky," I said. Then I glanced at my watch. "Yikes, Spencer! It's almost time for dinner. I'd better go. Besides, I can't wait to tell Dad!"

Chapter Three

● ● ● ● ●

"Zack, this ice cream is really good!" Dad said, looking up from his bowl of You Scream Eyes Scream. "No wonder you and Spencer are finalists."

"Thanks," I said. I'd had a bowl for dessert, too. Now, I know I said it before, but our flavour was dynamite. "The winner is going to be announced on Saturday. In just two days. The guy who called from the contest said—" I stopped talking. Dad was looking at me in a funny way.

"Dad, what's the matter?" I asked.

"Zack," he said, "are you feeling all right?"

"Fine. Great. Couldn't be better. Why do you ask?"

"Well, you look very pale." Dad peered at me more closely. "Well, not exactly pale. You actually seem to be . . . fading," he said. "As in becoming transparent."

"What?"

I ran to the bathroom and looked in the mirror. Dad was right. I did look kind of see-through – sort of cloudy, the way ghosts look in movies. "Oh, no!" I said. "The disappearing ink! Could it be?"

Dad followed me into the bathroom. "Zack, what are you talking about?" he said.

"I was at Spencer's today. You know how he's always making experiments. Well, I accidentally drank some disappearing ink," I said. "I thought it was lemonade."

"Hmm, disappearing ink," said Dad. He was quiet for a second. Then he said, "Well, that can't be too bad for you. Isn't it made mostly of lemon juice?"

I looked in the mirror again. I *was* fading right before my very own eyes. "Dad, this is serious. I think I'm disappearing."

"Oh, come on, Zack," Dad said. "Don't overreact. At the moment, you're just a little fuzzy, that's all."

"This is how it always starts," I said. "Now I'm just a *little* bit invisible. The same way I got a *little* bit catlike after getting scratched by that Egyptian statue. And the same way my teeth got a *little* bit crooked after I drank Dr Jekyll's crazy mouthwash. Then, before you know it – wham! – I've got a full-blown paranormal situation on my hands." I looked pleadingly at Dad. "Can't we at least talk to the doctor about this? I really think I need medical attention."

By the time we got to Dr. Kropotkin's office, I had faded even more. In the waiting room, I leafed through some old *National Geographics.* I noticed that I could read the one I was holding right through my fingers. That's hardly ever happened to me before. I was starting to feel a little panicky.

At last, the nurse said we could go in to see the doctor.

"Well, well, well," said Dr Kropotkin. "Hello, Zack. I haven't seen you in a while."

"I hope you can see him now," Dad said and laughed. He seemed to find this a lot funnier than I did.

"So," said the doctor, looking at his charts. "I just want to check your records.

Ah, yes. The last time you called, it seems you were turning into a cat."

"Right," I said.

He turned to look at me. "Well, you look as though you've recovered," he said.

"Yes, sir."

"How did I cure that, by the way? My records don't say."

"It wasn't you, sir," I said. "An Egyptian princess and I held a magic ceremony by the river. And that did the trick. The Egyptian princess turned into a cat instead of me."

"Ah, yes," said the doctor. It sounded like he'd heard of deals like that before. "So. What seems to be the trouble today?"

"Well," said Dad, "Zack accidentally drank some disappearing ink. It didn't bother him at first. But now he seems to be fading."

The doctor nodded seriously.

"They don't actually recommend that

you *drink* disappearing ink," said the doctor.

"It was an accident," I said. "I thought it was lemonade."

"Ah," said the doctor. "Well, let's take a look at you. We'll see what we can do."

The doctor gave me a complete examination. He took my pulse. He took my blood pressure. He listened to my heart with his stethoscope. He hit my knee with this little rubber hammer. He looked in my ears. He looked up my nose. He had me open my mouth and looked down my throat with a flashlight.

"Well," he said to Dad. "I can't really see anything wrong with this young man. To be perfectly honest, I can barely see him at all. Outside of that, he's a healthy, ten-year-old boy." Then he showed us out of his office.

On the way home, Dad tried to make me feel better. "It's true that strange things are always happening to you, Zack. But they always have a way of working out. Besides, you've been in worse situations than this." Dad chuckled. "At least you're not *completely* invisible."

Chapter
Four

● ● ● ● ●

When I woke up on Friday morning, I was completely invisible. I walked into the bathroom to brush my teeth, and I couldn't even find them to brush. When I looked in the bathroom mirror, nobody looked back at me. And when I put my clothes on, it looked like a shirt and a pair of trousers walking around without a body inside them. It was pretty spooky.

I begged Dad to let me stay home from

school. I could just imagine the comments I would get walking into class without a head. But Dad has a rule. Unless your temperature's over 100 degrees, you go to school. So I was going to school.

But before I did, I had to figure out a way to keep people from freaking out when they saw me. I saw this movie once where a man turned invisible. He wrapped bandages around his head and his hands to cover up the problem. He looked pretty weird. But at least he looked like *something.*

It was worth a try. I looked around the bathroom, found a roll of gauze, and started wrapping. And wrapping. I made sure to leave little holes for my eyes, my nose, and my mouth. By the time I had covered my head, I had just about used up the whole roll. Plus, I was almost late for school. So I grabbed a pair of gloves, sunglasses, and a baseball cap, which I shoved down on top of my bandaged head. No matter how ridiculous I looked, this would have to do.

Luckily, Spencer was the first person I saw at school. He was in the hallway getting stuff out of his locker. When he saw me walking towards him with my head all bandaged up, his eyes practically popped out of his head.

"Zack! Is that you?" said Spencer. "What happened? Your face?"

"It's that disappearing ink I drank," I said. "Underneath all this, I'm completely invisible."

"Oh my gosh!" Spencer cried. "You mean I actually made you disappear? I can't believe it. Can I take a peek?"

I nodded. Spencer lifted up a strip of gauze near my mouth. He looked like he was going to pass out.

"Spencer, you said nothing like this would happen."

"I guess I was wrong," he said. He shook his head. "I'm really sorry, Zack. I mean, this is an amazing scientific discovery. But I feel awful that this happened to you."

I sighed. "Well, it wasn't your fault," I said. "I was the one who drank the ink." Spencer and I headed for our classroom together. "I've just got to be visible by tomorrow for the contest," I said. "What if we win? How many chances does one kid get to be in *The New York Times*?"

"I know," said Spencer. He looked at me like I was some sort of really hard maths problem that he had to solve. "Don't worry, Zack. I'll try my best to figure something out."

Spencer and I got to class, but our teacher, Mrs Coleman-Levin, wasn't there yet. So far nobody had noticed me. That was because all the kids were standing around Vernon Manteuffel's desk. They were listening to him blabber on about something.

". . . and that's why, as of tomorrow," said Vernon, "I will be the grand prize winner in the Len and Larry's Create-an-Ice-Cream-Flavour Contest, and get free ice cream for a whole year!"

Spencer and I looked at each other. Then we looked back at Vernon.

"*You're* one of the finalists in the Len and Larry's Create-an-Ice-Cream-Flavour Contest?" Spencer asked.

Vernon turned around. "So? What's it to you, Spencer?" Vernon said. Then he did a double-take when he saw me. "Hey, who's that?" he added, pointing at me.

"It's me, Zack," I said.

"Gee, Zack," Vernon said, "didn't anyone tell you that Halloween is not until October?" Then he cracked up at his own joke.

"Very funny, Vernon," I said. I didn't

feel like explaining things to the whole class, so I didn't. "And it just so happens, Spencer and I are finalists in the ice-cream flavour contest, too."

"Then I bet I don't have a thing to worry about," said Vernon. "I'll bet you both a thousand dollars I'm going to win. And I've got the money, too."

Vernon is a jerk. He's really rich, and he never lets you forget it. When he's mad, he sits on you. Also, he sweats a lot. He sweats even in cold weather. Today he looked like Niagara Falls.

"Hey, Vernon," said one of the other kids. "What's your flavour, anyway?"

"That's top secret," Vernon said. "But it's better than Spencer and Zack's flavour, that's for sure. Which is lucky for you, Zack. If you won the contest, think of what you'd look like in the newspaper, all wrapped up like a mummy or something."

I hate to admit it. But Vernon was getting to me.

"For your information, Vernon," I said, "I'm wrapped up because I'm invisible. All right? If I didn't have these bandages on, you wouldn't be able to see any of me."

Vernon started laughing so hard I thought he was going to pass out. The other kids cracked up, too.

"Yeah, right," he said, after he caught his breath. "Invisible. I really believe that."

That was it. Vernon was so obnoxious. Without thinking, I took off my baseball cap and sunglasses. I felt around on my head for the end of the bandage.

Then I started unwrapping. Pretty soon I was standing in front of them, headless.

Let me tell you. No one was laughing now.

Vernon looked like his eyes were about to pop out. The sweat on his face was pouring out even faster than before.

That's when Mrs Coleman-Levin walked into the classroom. She's pretty cool. She's also weird, but in a nice way.

So when Mrs Coleman-Levin saw an empty set of clothes in her classroom, she didn't scream. She didn't even act very surprised. She just said in this very normal tone of voice, "Is that you, Zack?"

"Yes, it's me, Mrs Coleman-Levin. How did you know?" I said.

"Just a wild guess," she replied. "What did you do, drink disappearing ink?"

"Yes, ma'am," I said. "That's exactly what I did."

"Well, everybody, sit down," she said to all the kids. "You, too, Zack. Class is about to begin." She took a long look at me. "Hmmm. Zack, I don't know. How can I mark you present if I can't see you?"

"Well, you can't mark me absent," I said.

"That's true. Then I suppose I'll just

have to call on you a lot more in science today," she said. "It's the only way I can tell if you're paying attention."

Oh, great! Mrs Coleman-Levin was picking on me just because I was invisible. That wasn't fair. Invisible people have rights, too. If I could find some other invisible kids, we could get together and demand better treatment. The problem is, where would I go to find them?

"Mrs Coleman-Levin," I said, following her to her desk. "Have you ever heard of anybody becoming invisible before?"

"Of course," she said. "But it usually doesn't last long. It's like a suntan. After a few days, it goes away."

"Will I be back to normal by tomorrow?" I asked. "In a little more than twenty-four hours, the winners of the Len and Larry ice-cream contest will be announced. And if Spencer and I win, it would be sort of nice to be visible for the picture."

"Well, when I turned invisible, I got over it in only a day or two."

"*You* were invisible?" I said.

She nodded. "Not from drinking disappearing ink. So it's not quite the same situation. But I'm confident you'll figure something out, Zack. You always do."

Then Mrs Coleman-Levin went to the blackboard and started writing on it. She told everyone to open their science books to page sixty-seven. But there was no way I could concentrate. I quickly scribbled a note to Spencer:

Spencer, you're the genius. Have you thought of some way to get me back to normal?

I folded it up into a little square and checked to make sure Mrs Coleman-Levin wasn't watching. Then I tossed the note into his lap.

A couple of minutes later, he passed me a reply:

What about this? You know how faded clothes

need to be washed with colour-brightening detergent. Maybe you should soak in a bath with lots of Colour Brite detergent in it. My mom always buys the jumbo-sized boxes. So I know we have plenty at home.

I thought about it for a moment, then scribbled back:

It probably wouldn't work. There's no colour on me left to brighten.

Spencer chewed on the end of his pencil, then wrote:

Maybe I can brew up an anti-invisible ink potion for you to drink?

I almost choked when I read that one.

Are you crazy?!?! I'm never drinking another potion of yours ever again!!!

Spencer stared off into space for a while. I could almost see his huge IQ at work. Finally he smiled and leaned back in his chair. He tossed me the last note:

I do have one idea that may work. Come to my house after school.

Chapter
Five

● ● ● ● ●

"**O**K. This won't make you visible," Spencer said. "But at least maybe you'll look OK for tomorrow and the contest."

"Listen," I said. "I'm desperate. I'm willing to try anything."

I was sitting in Spencer's desk chair. As soon as school let out, we had rushed back to Spencer's house. He was going to put make-up all over my face.

Make-up? you ask.

Yes, make-up. Like I said, I was willing to

try anything. Spencer had one of those big face-painting kits open on his desk. He was using all the make-up to paint a face on me. He also had a Halloween wig and some sunglasses for me.

"Um, Zack, is this your nose or your chin?" Spencer asked, poking me for the fifteenth time.

"My nose!" I squeaked. "Look, are you sure you know what you're doing?"

"Of course," said Spencer. "I mixed some more white into the pink. And I got a very natural-looking skin tone. I'm even going to give you some freckles."

For some reason, I was getting a little worried. "Let me take a look," I said.

"No, no, no," Spencer said. "You can't look until I'm all done."

So I sat and picked at an invisible hangnail and thought about the contest instead. Even if we didn't win, I sure hoped Vernon wouldn't get the grand prize.

Vernon is the most obnoxious person I know. All day long, he kept saying how his flavour was so great. And how ours probably tasted like barf.

"Stop wrinkling your forehead, Zack," Spencer hissed at me. "Do you want to look like an old man?"

"I hate it that Vernon is one of the finalists," I said to Spencer. "If only we could taste his ice cream. Then we'd know if it was any good."

"Yeah," Spencer agreed. But I could tell he wasn't really listening. He was too busy fixing me up.

Finally, after about an hour, Spencer reached for the wig. It used to be part of a werewolf costume. But Spencer had cut it down a lot. He fitted it over my head.

"Almost done now. Just one last freckle and . . . ta da!" He spun the chair around so I faced the mirror.

I took one look . . . and screamed!

Chapter Six

● ● ● ● ●

"I look like a deranged freak!" I mean, think low-budget horror movie, or disgusting skin disease. I should have remembered art was never Spencer's strong point.

Spencer looked hurt. "I don't think it's so bad," he said.

"Look, I don't mean to make you feel bad." I patted Spencer on the shoulder. "But this is a face that would scare little children."

I grabbed a towel. Then I began

wiping the gunk off my face.

"Well, what are you going to do now?" Spencer asked.

"I don't know," I said. I sighed and wiped off the rest of the face paint.

Spencer began putting the make-up away. "It'll just kill me if Vernon wins," he said.

"Me too," I said. "If only we could try Vernon's flavour. Just a little taste. To see what the competition is." Then I got an idea. A great idea. I might be invisible, but there was nothing wrong with my brain.

"You know . . . there is a way I could," I said slowly.

"What do you mean?" Spencer asked. And then suddenly he knew what I was planning! "If you get completely undressed, nobody will see you. You can sneak into Vernon's apartment. Then you can find the ice cream and taste it."

I nodded and grinned. Then I realized Spencer couldn't see me. So I said, "My plan exactly."

I wasted no time getting undressed. I made Spencer turn around when I took off my boxers. Just in case.

Without my clothes on, I felt much breezier and cooler. It was a great feeling. I left Spencer's and went outside. I looked around. How weird. Nobody noticed me. Nobody knew there was a naked ten-year-old right in front of them. A fat lady in a flowered dress ploughed right into me.

"Hey, watch where you're going!" I yelled.

She jumped about three feet into the air.

If I had to be invisible, at least I might as well get some fun out of it.

In no time, I reached Vernon's house. He lived in a huge old building with a fancy canopy and a marble entrance. There was a doorman in a red uniform with gold trim. I slipped right by him and got in the elevator.

Soon I reached Vernon's floor. I rang the doorbell.

"Hello?" The butler opened the door. He looked up and down the hallway.

"Lousy kids," he grumbled. I almost burst out laughing as I sneaked in past him before he shut the door.

I headed for the kitchen. I knew where it was because I'd been to Vernon's before. You see, I once helped him get rid of a ghost – actually a poltergeist – that was living in his apartment. But that's another story.

Vernon was standing at the counter in the kitchen, talking to a guy in a white chef's uniform. The Manteuffels have their own private chef, in case I forgot to tell you.

"So, Philippe, did you make more ice cream for the contest tomorrow?" Vernon asked.

"It's all ready, sir," said Philippe.

"I think I need to taste it again," said Vernon.

"Very good, sir," said Philippe.

The chef went to the stainless steel refrigerator and opened the freezer. The freezer on Vernon's refrigerator is about the size of a Honda. He took out a big plastic bowl and removed the cover. I walked over and took a look. There it was. Vernon's contest entry!

The ice cream was green with little bits of candy in the shape of dollar signs. Very carefully, I inched over to the bowl and stuck my finger in it. One lick was all I wanted.

Now I've tasted mint ice cream before. But I've got to say that this was the *best* mint ice cream I'd ever had. This stuff wasn't great! It was spectacular.

"US Mint," said the chef. "Quite a clever name, if I do say so myself, sir."

Vernon was polishing off a whole bowl of ice cream.

"Philippe, you sure make great ice cream," he said with his mouth full.

"Thank you, sir," said the chef.

I couldn't believe it! Vernon hadn't done anything at all! It was all the chef – even the name. Vernon was a great big cheater!

Philippe dipped a spoon into the ice cream and took a taste himself.

"Maybe a tad more mint," he said.

"Whatever you say. You're the chef," Vernon said. "Oooh, I'm going to beat the pants off Zack and Spencer!"

"Indeed, sir," said Philippe.

I couldn't take any more of this. I headed for the kitchen door. Wait till I tell Spencer about this.

The last thing I heard as I left the kitchen was Philippe saying, "Please, sir. Do try not to sweat into the ice cream."

Chapter
Seven

● ● ● ● ●

It was Saturday morning. The big day. When I woke up, I didn't open my eyes right away. I lay in bed and concentrated on being visible. Sometimes, if you're trying to get visible again, it helps to do that. I don't know how I know that, I just do. Then I took a deep breath and opened my eyes. I slowly moved my hand in front of my face.

Nothing. No wrist, no hand, no fingers. Just an empty pyjama sleeve floating in front of me.

I went into the kitchen.

"Dad, my condition hasn't improved at all," I said.

"So I see," Dad said. He looked up from his newspaper and smiled. "But look on the bright side —"

"No, Dad! Do not say anything to try to cheer me up. The Len and Larry Ice-Cream Taste-Off is in . . ." I looked up at the kitchen clock ". . . exactly one hour and fourteen minutes. If Spencer and I win, there's no way I can go to accept our prize, or get my picture in the paper. And if we lose and Vernon wins, it will be the most unfair thing in the whole world."

Dad nodded. Last night I had told him all about spying on Vernon and his chef. He wanted to call the judges. But I talked to Spencer a long time about the whole mess. And Spencer and I finally agreed. Vernon was a cheater, all right. But we were not rats. Plus You Scream Eyes

Scream was a great flavour. We were standing by our product.

Dad made me blueberry pancakes – my favourite – to cheer me up. Then he told me to get undressed and we'd go. Because, of course, the only way I could go to the taste-off was stark naked.

Dad and I got to Len and Larry's early, but it was already a madhouse. A brass band was playing. Clowns with big shoes and red noses were handing out balloons. And people were dressed up in wacky costumes. One guy was dressed like an ice-cream cone. A whole bunch of people were bananas. A stage was set up at the back of the store. There were microphones, reporters, and photographers. There were banners saying, "Len and Larry's Grand Opening! New Flavour Taste-Off Today!"

Camera crews from the TV channels

were setting up big bright lights near the stage. I heard someone say that the winner was going to be on the six o'clock news!

I looked around for Spencer in the crowd. I didn't see him. But I did spot Vernon. He was there with his mom. He was sweating away like always. But he didn't look nervous. He looked like he was sure he had the prize in the bag.

Seeing Vernon got me boiling mad all over again. I wanted to get back at him some way. Then I got an idea. I was invisible, after all. I might as well take advantage of it.

I pushed through the crowd towards Vernon. I got real close to him and whispered in a low spooky voice.

"Vernon, this is your conscience speaking."

Vernon's eyes nearly bugged out of his head.

"It's wrong to cheat, Vernon. It is wrong

to say you created US Mint ice cream."

Now Vernon's eyes narrowed. "Zack?" he asked. "Is that you? It's you! I know it."

"Zack? Who is Zack?" I said in my low voice. "This is your conscience, Vernon."

"Oh, I know it's you, Zack!" he yelled. Vernon swatted at the air all around him. But I kept ducking away from him. "But how do you know I cheated? I mean . . . no, I'm not a cheater!" he said.

"I sneaked into your house and I saw the whole thing!" I shouted. "You're just a dirty rotten cheater!"

Vernon started punching the air wildly. I sidestepped his fists and pinched his nose.

"Ouch! I'll get you!" Vernon yelled.

"Vernon Aloysius Manteuffel, what are you doing?" his mother asked. She kept mopping her brow with a lace hanky. She's a big sweater, too. "People are staring. Stop it!"

"See you later, Vernon *Aloysius*!" I said.

Then I looked for Spencer. I wanted to wish us both luck before the judging. But I still didn't see him.

I inched my way closer to the stage. I had lost sight of Dad, too.

Before I had a chance to look further, two bearded men in pink-and-white striped overalls walked up to the mike. I'd know them anywhere. I've eaten dozens of pints of ice cream with their faces on the cartons. It was Len and Larry!

"Ladies and gentlemen," either Len or Larry said. "Welcome to the grand opening of our new ice-cream parlour and our Create-an-Ice-Cream-Flavour contest. We got so many great entries. But we were somehow able to narrow it down to six finalists. Will you please come up on stage?"

Now I saw Spencer making his way through the crowd from the other side of the room. I watched as he and Vernon and four other people lined up in a row on stage. They all looked pretty nervous. Vernon was sweating up a storm under the hot lights. Spencer looked like he was scanning the crowd, hoping to see me.

"Let's give everyone a big round of applause," said Len or Larry.

"Now it's time for the taste-off," said Len or Larry. "Here are our judges – all experts in the field of frozen dessert treats. They will take one last taste before they pick a winner."

The three judges were very stern looking. Each clutched a sterling silver ice-cream spoon in his hand. Not one cracked a smile. It looked as if they took their frozen dessert treats very seriously. I had a bad feeling they weren't going to like ice cream with wobbly eyeballs in it.

They first stopped in front of a bowl of ice cream labelled Sweets for the Sweet.

The first judge took a big spoonful. "It has a delicate flavour that reminds me of early-vintage Bazooka," he said.

"It's fresh, lively, and complex," said the second.

"It has a sweet, full-bodied personality," agreed the third.

Then the judges moved on to Yes, We Have No Bananas, vanilla ice cream with everything, except for, you guessed it, bananas. After that came Cherry Seinfeld and Death by Way-Too-Much Chocolate. Nobody seemed too crazy about any of them. So now it was Vernon's turn with US Mint.

"Superior!" they all cried. "It's smooth, rich, and polished."

The third judge nodded. "It finishes off with some very snappy mint tones."

The first two judges nodded excitedly.

Vernon grinned and sweated.

I groaned. They loved US Mint!

I held my breath as the judges sampled our entry. Spencer looked like he was going to throw up, he was so nervous.

It took a long time before they said anything. "It is surprising and intense," the first judge said slowly.

The second judge nodded. "The strawberry tingles the taste buds in a strange way."

"The eyeballs add an unusual raw texture," remarked the third.

Huh? Did they like it or not? Spencer looked as confused as I felt.

The judges went into a huddle. I could see them arguing. Then they seemed to come to an agreement. They wrote something down, put it in an envelope, and handed it to Len and Larry.

Len and Larry walked over to the mike. "We have a winner," said Len or Larry. He opened the envelope. "And now the moment you've all been waiting for. And the winner is . . . You Scream Eyes Scream!"

"No way!" I screamed. "We won! I can't believe it. We won!"

Everybody turned in the direction of my shouts. But nobody could see me, of course. Spencer stepped forward. He looked like he was in shock.

Here was my big moment, and I was going to miss it. I jumped onstage. Len or Larry was handing Spencer a giant-sized cheque about the size of a beach towel. It was for a hundred dollars!

I squeezed Spencer's arm. "I'm right here with you, buddy! We won!" I whispered.

"Zack? Zack!" Spencer still looked dazed. "I can't believe it."

It was hot on the stage. Very hot. And the lights were so bright I had to squint.

"Congratulations, young man," said Len or Larry. He shook Spencer's hand

and handed him the cheque. "But where is your co-creator?"

"Um, thank you," said Spencer. He cleared his throat and stepped up to the mike. "I'm only sorry that Zack couldn't be here this morning to share this moment with me."

Spencer turned in my direction. There was a huge smile on his face. Then his look changed. He gasped.

"Uh-oh," he said.

What was the matter?

"Look at you," he said.

He pointed. I looked. Oh no! The outlines of my body were very faint. Like a jellyfish in the ocean. Like a ghost in the fog. But I could see me. And I was filling in fast!

I was becoming visible again! I had been waiting for two days for this to happen. Talk about terrible timing! Why now?

Spencer looked at me again. Then he smacked himself on the forehead. "Of course!" he said. "It's so obvious!"

"Huh?" I said as my feet slowly began to materialize. My *naked* feet.

"It's the heat from all the TV lights!" said Spencer. "Just like when I held the invisible ink up to the hot desk-lamp bulb. So simple – yet I didn't figure it out."

"I've got to get out of here!" I yelped. "Or else I'm going to be butt-naked in front of all these people!"

Chapter Eight

● ● ● ● ●

The people closest to the stage were beginning to notice. I saw Dad shouting and pointing at me. I grabbed the humungous cheque out of Spencer's hands. I held it in front of me and went racing off the stage.

But that left my rear end unprotected. People behind me started to laugh and shout. They had no idea who I was. They must have thought I was a streaker or something. I had to cover myself front and back! As quickly as possible!

"Excuse me! Coming through!" I shouted. I pushed my way through a bunch of people and ran around to the back of the stage. The first thing I saw was a door marked *Dressing Room*. I opened it and ducked for cover.

There was no one else inside. Whew. I looked around for some kind of big coat or something – anything that would cover me. Bingo! On a chair right in front of me was a pile of clothes. I grabbed this bright yellow robe-type thing, and I threw it on. It fitted strangely, with some sort of hood that stuck up a little and no real sleeves. But I wanted to get right back out onto the stage for the picture, so I just zipped up the front, and ran outside.

I made it back up on stage and raced over next to Spencer just as the *New York Times* photographer was getting ready to snap the picture.

"All right, you two. Just look right here and say, 'Cheese!'"

The flash bulb went off.

Then the entire crowd started laughing and pointing at me. I looked down at the yellow thing I had put on, and I understood why.

Well, Spencer and I did get our picture in *The New York Times*. But it wasn't quite what I'd had in mind. Still, I guess being in a banana suit was better than being in my birthday suit.

You Scream Eyes Scream became a big hit, by the way. It's sold in practically every supermarket. But if you can't find some where you live, you can always drop by and see me. (And you can see me now, because I am 100% totally visible.) I'll treat you to some You Scream Eyes Scream. I always have a gallon in the freezer.

THE ZACK FILES

Read all of Zack's weird adventures!

All Macmillan titles can be ordered at your local bookshop
or are available by post from:

**Book Service by Post
PO Box 29, Douglas, Isle of Man IM99 1BO**

Credit cards accepted. For details:
Telephone: 01624 675137
Fax: 01624 670923
E-mail: bookshop@enterprise.net

Free postage and packing in the UK.
Overseas customers: add £1 per book (paperback)
and £3 per book (hardback).

The prices shown are correct at the time of going to press. However,
Macmillan Publishers reserve the right to show new retail prices on
covers which may differ from those previously advertised.